ABC
of Canada

For our parents, Bev and Brian, Peter and Christine — K.B. and P-H.G.

Text © 2002 Kim Bellefontaine
Illustrations © 2002 Per-Henrik Gürth

Kids Can Press acknowledges the financial support of the Government of
Ontario, through the Ontario Media Development Corporation's Ontario Book
Initiative; the Ontario Arts Council; the Canada Council for the Arts; and the
Government of Canada, through the BPIDP, for our publishing activity.

Published in Canada by	Published in the U.S. by
Kids Can Press Ltd.	Kids Can Press Ltd.
29 Birch Avenue	2250 Military Road
Toronto, ON M4V 1E2	Tonawanda, NY 14150

www.kidscanpress.com

The artwork in this book was created in Adobe Illustrator.
The text is set in Providence-Sans Bold.

Edited by Jennifer Stokes and Debbie Rogosin
Designed by Per-Henrik Gürth and Julia Naimska
Printed and bound in China

The hardcover edition of this book is smyth sewn casebound.
The paperback edition of this book is limp sewn with a drawn-on cover.

CM 02 0 9 8 7 6
CM PA 04 0 9 8

National Library of Canada Cataloguing in Publication Data

Bellefontaine, Kim (Kim Anne)
          ABC of Canada

ISBN 978-1-55337-340-7 (bound).
ISBN 978-1-55337-685-9 (pbk.)

1. Alphabet — Juvenile literature. 2. Canada — Juvenile literature.

I. Gürth, Per-Henrik II. Title.

PE1155.B43 2002   j421'.1   C2001-901518-

Kids Can Press is a *corus* Entertainment company

ABC
of Canada

illustrated by
Per-Henrik Gürth

written by
Kim Bellefontaine

Kids Can Press

A a

is for Arctic,
in the icy cold north.

B b
is for Beaver,
busy building a dam.

C c

is for Calgary Stampede —
days of rodeo fun. Yee haw!

D d

is for Dogsled,
gliding across the snow.

F f

is for Flag,
waving in a parade.

G g

is for Geese,
flying south
for the winter.

H h

is for Hockey —
he shoots, he scores!

I i

is for Ice Fishing,
on a frozen lake. Brrr!

J j

is for Jasper National Park,
in the heart of the Rocky
Mountains.

K k

is for Kayak,
skimming across
the bay.

L l

is for Lobster,
snapping its
claws.

O o

is for Ottawa,
the capital
city of Canada.

Q q
is for Quebec
City — take a
carriage ride!

R r

is for Royal
Canadian Mounted
Police — see the
Mountie on
the horse.

T t

is for Toronto,
Canada's largest
city.

V v

is for Vancouver,
city by the ocean.

X x

is for X-Country Skiing,
through the snowy woods.

Y y
is for Yukon, where the
Northern Lights glow.

Z z

is for Zamboni,
cleaning the ice.